The Commandment

Loreli Love

Published by Loreli Love, 2021.

THE COMMANDMENT

First edition. October 20, 2021.

ISBN: 979-8201399160

Written by Loreli Love.

Also by Loreli Love

The Education of Charlotte Royce
The Commandment
Tempting Tina: An Impossible Erotic Romance
Sailing for Santa Lucia: an Erotic Odyssey
The Governess: An Erotic Regency Romance Novel
The Earl's Lady
The Divination of Tamara Knightly: an Erotic Regency
Romance
The Quartet's Quandary: an Erotic Regency Romance

Table of Contents

Chapter 1- Temptation

You know that commandment, one of the Ten, the one that says "Thou shalt not covet thy neighbor's wife"? Well, I broke it, or a variation of it.

In my case, you could say something more like I coveted my husband's brother. And I was punished. Perhaps not as harshly as I could have been, but when you've tasted ecstasy, when you have been to the moon, how much more difficult it is to come back to earth and endure the travails of everyday life!

It all started when I became engaged to my husband. Our families were ecstatic over such a union, because the combined wealth and power of our marriage would greatly enhance the prestige and the glory of both families. I was happy to make my family happy, and I'm sure James felt the same way. He was such a good soul, so kind, so caring, and so considerate.

I first met him at one of the tea dances my mother loved to throw at our summer home in the Catskills. I'd just turned nineteen the day before and I was walking on a cloud. My brother Barry and my sister Katherine had both invited friends of theirs and we were a full house that afternoon, dancing on the lawns sloping down to the lake. James Wentworth Kensington was the oldest boy in the Kensington clan. Katherine had pointed him out to me along with all the other young men she had her eye on. She was only seventeen and still too young for the marriage mart, but it didn't down slow her interest.

Historically, I hadn't much cared for boys. I preferred riding and caring for my horse, Nick. But that afternoon, I knew as the oldest daughter, and one who had now reached her maturity at nineteen, I would make Mama and Papa most happy if I began the necessary process of finding a husband.

Barry introduced me to James, and minutes later, he held me in his arms as we danced across the grass. He was tall, with dark brown hair and blue eyes, and he was handsome, but no more so than my own brother or any of the other young men at the parties. The thing about James was that he was such a kind soul. And I felt he really liked me. It wasn't that phony flirtatiousness that so many young men had thrown my way. He was sincere. And, it made me able to be sincere back to him.

So, after a short courtship, we were to be married. Together, our families threw an enormous engagement ball at the Kensington mansion in New York. Everything was going just as planned until the first dance. As the guests of honor, James and I led out the dance. We twirled about the room, my white gown floating over James's black tuxedo-clad legs, when I felt someone staring at me. The sensation wasn't surprising since everyone was watching us, but something drew my eyes to one edge of the crowd. A tall, broad-shouldered man leaned against one of the massive columns supporting the ballroom. His arms were crossed against his chest, and I felt compelled to meet his gaze. His hair was brown, with blond streaks, and swirled in loose curls about his head. Beneath that crown of hair, twin beams of green light seemed to beckon me.

All through the dance, I felt his eyes on me, measuring me, assessing me, calling to me. And even before James guided me to his side, I knew this must be Thomas, James's younger brother. It was there in the cut of his jaw-line and in the proud way that he carried himself.

THE COMMANDMENT

"My dear, may I introduce you to my brother, Thomas?" James relinquished my hand to that disturbing man. "Thomas, this is Sarah Pughes Wilson, my fiancée."

His hand was huge and warm and closed over mine in an intimate grasp that made my knees weak. I barely heard James explain that Thomas had been abroad, seeking his fortunes in Africa, and that he had returned home for the wedding. When Thomas brought my hand to his lips, I couldn't tear my eyes away from the erotic image of his masculine mouth, the firm yet sensual curve of his lips, pressing on the smooth white skin on the back of my hand.

I felt heat rising from somewhere deep inside and when his green eyes rose slowly, caressingly over the low cut of my ball gown and met mine, I found myself blushing like a maiden and not the mature nineteen year old I was.

"My pleasure, Miss Wilson." His hand squeezed mine before releasing it.

It was all I could do to keep from gasping, as I felt the sure, firm stroke of his thumb over my palm. His forest green eyes never left mine and I found myself unable to speak. I simply nodded, helpless in my response to the masculine hunger glowing in those remarkable eyes.

"Would you like to dance with her?" I vaguely heard James ask his brother and the next thing I knew, Thomas had swept me away in a waltz.

He was similar to James and yet so incredibly different. I felt safe with James, safe and secure, but with Thomas, I felt like a deer being hunted by a tiger or a lion. He was so big, and he held me with such force and power against him.

"My brother is a lucky man," Thomas said and pulled me closer. "As lucky as he's always been."

I pushed discreetly against his chest and tried to put a little distance between us. It was almost immodest how close he was holding me, and I didn't want anyone to comment.

"Please," I whispered under my breath.

"What was that?" He dipped his head.

"Sir!" I gasped as I felt his lips brush my ear and 1 tilted my head back, away from his dangerous mouth. But that made me look up into his dangerous eyes.

"You are so young, so innocent," he said.

The next thing I knew, he was twirling me out through the large French doors and onto the terrace. As I spun, I saw James speaking with his father, and my Mama and Papa were similarly engaged. I hoped to God that no one saw Thomas take me from the room.

"How old are you?" he asked once we were outside.

"Please, release me." I repeated my request and pushed again at his broad shoulders.

"Not until you tell me your age." His teeth were very white in the dark.

"I'm nineteen, but I don't see how it's any of your business." I thrust my head back to challenge him, only realizing after the fact that the action also pushed my breasts more firmly against his chest.

"Old enough for me," he said and swept his mouth down over mine.

What can I say?

James had kissed me, delicate butterfly kisses on my wrists, my palms, and the back of my hands. He'd once grasped me in his arms and pressed an ardent kiss against my closed mouth, and then had apologized profusely for having lost control.

But that was no comparison to this.

This was fire and liquid and melting heat. His lips closed over mine and when I gasped in surprise and startled outrage, his tongue slipped into my mouth, penetrating me with strong slick thrusts. Honest to God, I felt like I was going to faint. My knees went weak and I sagged in his arms.

The next thing I knew, he'd whisked me off the terrace and into the gardens. I was still gasping for breath when he pushed me up against the garden wall and I felt his hands roaming along the sides of my body.

I would have done something, perhaps screamed for help, but his mouth had renewed its passionate assault on mine. I couldn't think, I couldn't object, I couldn't free myself from his outrageous assault. All I could do was hang onto his shoulders to keep from collapsing.

His knee pressed between my legs, pushing high at the cleft of my thighs. Oh heavens, I felt on fire and wet moisture slicked my body where it slid on his rock-hard thigh. When one of his hands lifted and closed over my breast, I felt tension rising, spiraling, twisting out of control within my body. And though I knew that I was engaged to another man, that I must remain chaste until the marriage bed, I could not help the violent passion ripping through my body.

He cupped and shaped cand squeezed my breast, all while his tongue kept up its slick thrusting and retreat from my mouth, his thigh ramming more fully against my delicate flesh, forcing my legs wider apart.

When he took my nipple between his thumb and forefinger and began to squeeze and roll it firmly, I screamed into his mouth and felt the world go black around me. I would have fallen if it hadn't been for his long arm wrapped around my waist and the firm press of his body supporting me against the garden wall.

I spilled across his thigh and sank against his chest. He finally released me.

"What have you done?" I stared at him with wide, shocked eyes, still breathless from the sensations he had pulled from my body.

"Come, we must return to the ball." He guided me back into the warm room that was hot from the chandeliers and the dancing bodies. His arm was like steel around my waist.

Moments later, he'd disappeared into the crowd and I was left to find James. I couldn't go right away. I had to make sure I looked acceptable and I needed time to compose myself. I went to the powder room and stared in the mirror.

The woman who looked back was nothing like the young lady I'd been earlier this evening when I dressed for the ball. My eyes glowed with electric blue fire and they seemed much darker, more mysterious. My lips were redder and I could see where his mouth had rubbed the skin almost raw. I could still taste him on my tongue, an indescribable, delectable blend of man and wine. My legs still quivered and I felt my body pulsing deep inside. Thomas.

Just the thought of what he'd done to me and the moisture renewed its flow, wetting my petticoats.

THE COMMANDMENT

Stop it! I told myself, furious that I was allowing a man, obviously a rake, to have such an affect on me. I washed my face, fixed my hair, and pasted a bland smile on my face.

I returned to the ballroom and spent the rest of the evening with my civilized fiancé and our families. Thomas had disappeared, but I was too afraid to ask anyone where he might have gone. James never noticed, never suspected, a thing. As I said, he was a kind, caring, and trusting soul. Besides, there was no way I could or would compromise the commitment I'd made to him and to our families. T here was too much at stake in our union.

But I still thought of Thomas, and with each forbidden memory, my body burned with guilty pleasure.

I learned discreetly over the few days before the wedding that Thomas stood to inherit little of the family wealth. James and he had two sisters and another brother, but they were still children. This information clarified for me what Thomas had said and why he'd done what he had to me. He was jealous of his older brother.

Ashamed and guilty though I felt, I still was disappointed to realize he had only kissed me out of spite for his brother and not due to any attraction he had for me.

As the wedding preparations were put in place, I only hoped Thomas would keep himself away from me and I wouldn't have to see him after my marriage to James. Like clockwork, the wedding took place and all our families and friends were in attendance. I stayed away from Thomas which was not hard to do with so many people milling about the mansion.

The wedding transpired and hours later I found myself dressed in the sheer wedding nightgown my mother and sister had sewn for me. I lay on the bed and waited, my heart in my throat, knowing that I was about to consummate my marriage with James. The door sounded and my heart leapt.

"Come in." My voice was breathless, and I licked dry lips.

"So we are finally alone." James entered the room, turned and locked the door behind him. He was dressed in a long crimson velvet dressing gown. "You are so beautiful, my dear," he said and lowered himself onto the bed beside me. "Do you know how many days, and nights, I have thought of this moment?"

He took my hand, turned it over, and pressed delicate butterfly kisses across my wrist and into the center of my palm.

"James, kiss me," I said, and raised my face to him.

His mouth settled on mine, and he gently kissed me, his lips moving lightly across mine.

Unbidden, memories of Thomas's masterful kiss leapt to my mind and I could not help myself from wondering if my husband would deepen the kiss.

But he kept nibbling and kissing me with a closed mouth. Impatient, I opened my mouth slightly and let my tongue touch his lower lip. He pulled back startled, but then his blue eyes darkened and he smiled.

"You are not afraid?" he asked.

"Oh no, James. I want us to be man and wife. I want to have your children."

"Yes, yes," he groaned and climbed over me awkwardly. There was none of the assurance or mastery Thomas had exercised. It occurred to me that perhaps my husband was as little schooled in the world of human procreation as I was.

My experience with Nick and the other horses and animals at our country homes had taught me the basic mechanics of how to reproduce, but I had never seen a human male's anatomy, and I wasn't too sure where he should put it.

"My dear, I love you so much. You are everything I could desire." James knelt over me and studied my face. His face had darkened to a deep red and his eyes were almost black. He reached forward and placed his hands on my breasts. "I have always wanted to do this," he sighed and lowered himself over me.

I had to spread my legs so that he could lie down. He propped himself up on his elbows and gently traced the slopes of my breasts. I felt some hard part of him poke against my belly and I wondered if that was his manhood. He leaned down to kiss me some more and this time his tongue pushed tentatively between my lips. I tightened my mouth around his tongue and he groaned with pleasure. His hips surged instinctively forward and that rigid part of him began to thrust persistently against my belly. I reached up and ran my hands through his hair as he kissed me and stroked my breasts.

It felt good, it felt right. I knew that this was how my marriage night should be, and I felt satisfied that my husband would be a good and considerate lover, as he had been with his wooing. His hands left my breasts and he slowly slid my nightgown up.

"I want to make this good for you," he said breathlessly. "We will have beautiful children."

His gown parted and 1 felt his legs hairy against mine. The hard male flesh of him felt hot and smooth against my inner thigh. He adjusted his hips and his penis pushed against my tender flesh. He reached down with his hand and pushed himself more firmly against me. His chest pressed down heavily against mine, the fabric of my night gown rough as it rubbed against my breasts.

Both of us were breathing hard and fast. I felt excitement at consummating our marriage, but no one had prepared me for the excruciating pain that was to follow.

"Oh James," I gasped, feeling as if he were splitting me asunder.

"Sarah!" He thrust heavily forward and I felt his penis break through my maidenhead and bury itself deep inside me.

He was breathing heavily. His face and neck were wet with sweat against my forehead and the tight sensation between my legs began to disappear. He thrust once, twice, and then moisture flooded out and down between the crease of my rear and onto the sheets.

I felt his body slip free of me and I felt hollow with him no longer inside me. He kissed me lightly once more on the mouth and levered himself off me.

"I'm sorry if that hurt, my sweet. My father warned me that the first time can be difficult for a lady." He pulled his nightshirt down and wrapped the robe back around himself, but not before I saw his penis lying nested in black hair and his testicles a dark shadow behind. "I will call your maid." He pulled the bell rope and I pulled the covers over me. "I will return when you are ready," he said.

The maid came and quickly stripped the sheets and washed me. I felt happy and satisfied to know that even now I could be carrying James's child and that we had satisfactorily consummated our marriage. The maid smiled shyly at me and congratulated me as well.

When James returned, I wore my usual cotton nightgown. He removed his robe and wearing his nightshirt came to bed. I saw his penis poking out from his shirt and when he held me close as we fell asleep I could feel it pulsing swiftly, firmly against the plump flesh of my rear through my nightgown. The sensation wasn't unpleasant. In fact, I felt moisture pooling between my legs and I moved restlessly in his arms.

"James?" I whispered.

"Yes, my sweet, what is it?"

I was embarrassed to ask, but I took a deep breath and worked up the nerve. "Can we make love again?"

He chuckled, his breath warm against my hair and I felt his body seem to push even more tightly against my rear. "Maybe tomorrow. But, we've both had a long day and I've caused you enough pain for one night."

He spoke reasonably and I knew he was right, but as I drifted off to sleep, I found myself wondering if Thomas would be so reasonable.

***

Chapter 2 - Ecstasy

My marriage with James was everything a young lady of affluent means could desire.

We had a massive country house and a townhouse in the city. My sister and Mama were frequent visitors, as were James's parents and younger siblings. James was quite busy helping his father manage the Kensington properties, which were extensive and covered several states. His work and his travels kept him away from home for weeks on end, but when he was home, he never failed to consummate his marriage with me. We both hoped for children and after that first painful experience I came to enjoy our mating. It was nothing like the sensations I'd felt with his brother, but there was a comfort and a happiness that came from having him inside me, filling me with his seed.

Summer came, and with it the heat. We agreed that I should stay in the cooler climes of our country house than remain in the sweltering heat of New York City. James promised he would come up as often as he could get away. In the meantime, my Mama and sister promised they would come as soon as they could.

I found myself arriving at the country home late one afternoon in June with my maid. The place had been readied for me by the groundskeeper, and a cook had been hired for the summer. I went up to my room, thankful to rest after the long and sweltering journey. The maid had gone down to the kitchen and I was alone.

I removed my outer dress and stood in my chemise and corset and looked out into the forest surrounding the estate. It was so beautiful, so tranquil and thankfully cool. I let my hair down from the scratchy pins and enjoyed the silken flow of my long blond hair over my shoulders. The door creaked as it swung open. I assumed it was the maid.

"That was quick, Hetty," I said.

"We meet again."

I spun around at the sound of that familiar, deep voice. My eyes flew to his but Thomas was not looking at my face. I felt the scarlet flush creep up my neck and I wrapped my hands around my chest, trying to preserve my modesty.

"What are you doing here?" I rushed over to seize my dressing gown. Anything to cover myself from his probing green eyes.

"Not so fast." His arm snaked out and he stopped me before I'd moved one foot. "I think I prefer you like this."

He hauled me against him and his green eyes dropped to my cleavage, made more pronounced by his chest pressed against mine.

"Thomas, you mustn't. I'm married to your brother." I wet nervous lips as I saw the fierce hunger coloring his high cheekbones and how his eyes had darkened.

"Ah James. How is my dear brother?" His hand moved down and with one finger he lightly traced the tops of my breasts where they mounded naked above the bodice of the chemise.

"Please, stop, sir." I tried to twist away from him, but he ruthlessly grabbed my hand in one of his massive hands and pressed them deep into my back, pushing me more firmly against him.

With his other hand, he continued to trace the tops of my breasts. Heaven help me, but once again I felt the wild flutter of desire pulse through me. I felt the thick rigid press of his male flesh stabbing against my belly. I swallowed, my mouth suddenly as dry as cotton.

"That's not going to happen, Sarah. Has my brother pleasured you like I have? Has he touched you like this?"

Forgive me, James, forgive me God, but when his hand ripped the bodice open and his hand closed over my naked breast I could do nothing but close my eyes and pant in helpless response, my breath swelling my lungs and heaving my bosom more deeply into his hand.

Oh, and when his thumb and forefinger began their merciless torment of my nipple, I felt my knees weaken.

"Please," I managed to say, even as a river of moisture poured down my thighs.

"Please, what? More of this?" Thomas released my hands and I grabbed his waist to keep from collapsing.

Both his hands went to my breasts and continued their sensual assault. I looked down, both ashamed and secretly titillated by the sight. His hands were large, but so were my breasts. Mama had been so proud when my bosom had begun to grow, but she'd not expected them to swell to such a size. I'd found them cumbersome when I rode Nick, their bouncing uncomfortable.

But now, oh God. Now, they burned with fire and need.

"You like this, don't you?" he muttered under his breath and lowered his head.

Oh heavens! His mouth closed around one peaked nipple and I felt that same dizziness I'd felt once before.

James had never done such a thing. In fact, James had never seen me without my nightgown. It simply wasn't what was done between properly married people, at least between us.

"Thomas, you need to, ahhh—-" The gush of pleasure was unexpected and burst over me like fireworks. My legs gave out and the next thing I knew, I lay across Thomas's lap on the bed.

"You are incredible. So responsive, so beautiful." He looked down at me.

I lay languid in the aftermath across his lap. His hands had resumed their caresses of my naked breasts. My chemise was down to my waist.

"You're practically glowing," he said and dropped his mouth once more to my throbbing nipple. His tongue worked wickedly over my flesh and helplessly I began to squirm once more against him.

"Sir, Thomas. You mustn't," I protested, but only half-heartedly. I could barely speak much less breathe as I felt his hand tweaking my nipple, pulling and squeezing endlessly and then I felt his teeth close around the other nipple. He bit down.

"Oh God!" I cried out and sensation ripped through me once more.

Before I could recover, his mouth was on mine, his tongue thrusting deep into my mouth. And heaven help me, but I opened for him, I accepted his hungry male demands.

But then there came a knock on the door. I froze, desperately aware of the compromising position I was in. Thomas seemed completely in control of himself and instantly removed me from his lap, retrieved the dressing gown and wrapped it around me.

"I will see you later," he said and pressed a last hard kiss to my lips.

"Just a minute, Hetty," I called as Thomas left through the door into the master's suite.

The master's suite, what a joke. My husband, his brother's suite! But there wasn't time to think or react. I simply had to get off the bed and let Hetty in. So I did.

And when she was gone, I carefully mended the chemise so that no evidence remained of Thomas's behavior, except for the rosy pulsing in my breasts and the wet throbbing deep in my belly.

James had arranged for Nick to be transported to our country home. It was with some relief that I later dressed to ride and headed down to the stables. I needed to get away from the confines of the house, from the evidence of my marriage, and from any chance that Thomas might once again try something with me.

Nick was just as eager as I to be free, and we galloped out of the barn and onto the road that led away from Haven Home. I rode for an hour, thinking about James and his brother and about my marriage. I loved James. He was my husband and hopefully would soon be the father of my children, but as the sun sank below the tops of the pine trees and the air was thick with the smell of pine and vanilla, I had to admit that his brother had a hold over me. Simply thinking his name was enough for heat to rise up from between my thighs, and when I remembered how he touched my bare breasts, the saddle became almost more than I could bear as it rubbed intimately against me.

Finally, I had to turn back, for dinnertime was approaching. I led Nick to his stable and dismissed the stable hand. I liked to curry Nick myself. I brushed him down and then went to the tack room to find a pick. I bent over the pile of tackle to find what I needed, when I heard the door shut behind me.

Before I could turn around, two big hands seized my hips and pulled me backwards against a hard male body. I tried to straighten up.

"Stay like you are." A big hand pushed between my shoulder blades and forced me back over. It was Thomas.

"Thomas, please. I have to finish with Nick and the stable hand is somewhere outside." I tried to straighten again, but gasped, when I felt him shoving my skirts up around my hips. "What, what are you doing?"

I tried to shift away, but he forced his groin firmly against me and my face was jammed into a pile of rags. I could feel his penis prodding between my legs. I could not see it, I had never even seen my husband's penis erect, but Thomas's seemed huge, pendulous, reminiscent of the stallions I had seen. The thought skittered through me and my heart leapt into my throat.

"Relax, you know you want it." His deep voice was little more than a rasp.

Both of his hands were on my ass. He'd pushed my skirts out of the way and his hands were warm and firm through the flimsy material of my underwear. He kneaded each lobe of my ass, and I found myself unable to do anything but squirm. His hands wouldn't stop their ceaseless kneading and I began to slide with wetness against my underwear.

"I sent the stable hand on an errand. Do you like that?" He arched over me.

I could feel him all along my back and his mouth was on my ear. He began to chew. "Tell me you like this, Sarah."

He stuck his tongue in my ear and blew in it. His hands had moved from my ass and now had resumed their torment of my breasts.

"Thomas, you mustn't," I said under my breath, but it was a fainthearted objection.

He squeezed my nipples once more, hard, rolling them, releasing them, cupping my breasts.

"You are incredible. So large, my hands can't contain you."

He licked my ear and then bit my neck as he rolled my nipples with his fingers and squeezed them some more. I moaned, the sensation almost bordering on pain as he squeezed and rubbed my nipples into aching points that stabbed against his palms. I could feel his penis, enormous through the loose folds of his pants, now rubbing between the lobes of my ass. At any second, I expected him to commit adultery with me. I had to do something!

"I'm married to your brother." I said it as much to remind myself as remind him of our filial responsibilities.

But fortunately, it must have meant something to him, because with a curse, he pushed himself away from me. I stood up and quickly shook out my skirts. I spun around to face him and saw his forest green eyes staring at my breasts. I knew he could see them erect from his attentions and poking through the material of my riding habit. His jaw clenched and I saw him flex his fists at his sides.

"My brother is so damned lucky," he growled and turned away.

Seconds later I was once again alone in the tack room. I sank down onto a bench and let out a breath I didn't even know I was holding. How close he'd come to violating the sanctity of my marriage! I couldn't lie to myself. I had not offered much objection. I sank my head into my hands and cried. What on earth was going to become of me?

When I made it back to the house, I was firmly composed. I had determined that no matter what, I would resist Thomas from now on. I owed it to James and I owed it to my future children. There was no way I would bear a bastard. I would not shame James, our families, or myself in such a manner. It was with great relief that I discovered Mama and Katherine had arrived for their visit.

"How marriage is agreeing with you, my dear!" Mama wrapped me in her ample embrace.

I blushed, happy to see her but unable to clarify her assumption. There was no way I could ever admit to her or to anyone else about what had transpired between myself and my husband's brother.

"Come, let us go inside," I said after hugging Katherine as well.

They were both pleasantly surprised to discover that Thomas was joining us for dinner. Neither thought it odd in the slightest that he was there. And he himself was quite glib in his explanation.

"James wanted me to arrange the purchase of several mares and cattle with Mr. Cassels. He also has a spectacular stallion that we've agreed to purchase stud rights to."

With those words, his green eyes met mine in an intimate glance and the message he secretly sent me caused my pulse to flutter. His eyes dropped to my breasts and I knew without a doubt he was remembering our earlier encounters. I knew I must not encourage him, so I looked away, but I was helpless in my body's reaction. His eyes on me felt like a caress and I felt my nipples instinctively respond, stabbing against the thin material of my gown.

That night, I made sure to lock both my bedroom doors. And the night after, and the night after. By the third day, I began to breathe a little easier in the hopes that Thomas knew how dangerous it would be to try something with my family all around. I had a wonderful time with my Mama and Katherine. It was almost like old times, except for when Mama cornered me alone at the breakfast table one morning.

"My dear, I have a question of the most delicate nature to put to you," she began.

My heart leapt in my throat when I thought she'd discovered my indiscretion, but then she continued and I relaxed.

"You and James have now been married almost three months. Forgive me, but it's only my motherly interest that provokes me."

"What is it, Mama?" I took a sip of cocoa.

"Are you yet with child, my dear?"

I blushed involuntarily. I couldn't help it. The question was of such an intimate nature.

"I'm not sure," I replied.

Over breakfast, she quickly and concisely explained all the details of pregnancy. I was thankful for the explanation, even as some perverse part of me realized that now I knew there were times when I was less fertile. That perverse part of my brain whispered that if Thomas were to take me then, I would not risk bearing a bastard.

Good heavens! What was I thinking?

THE COMMANDMENT

There were only five more days before James would return and I couldn't wait. The anxiety and fear surrounding Thomas was wearing me down. I looked forward to the safety and security I felt with my husband.

***

Chapter 3 - Returning Favors

The next morning, I went for a walk through the formal gardens of Haven Home. It was a gorgeous day with not a cloud in sight. I reached the end of the gravel walk at the far end of the garden and began the turn, when a big hand reached out through the trees and hauled me into the forest.

"Thomas!" I exclaimed in dismay as he pulled me after him, deeper into the woods. "Stop it, I must go back."

I tried to twist my hand free of his grasp but he yanked me forward and I stumbled.

"It's been too long," he said and swept me up into his arms.

I had vowed to fight him and so I put up a valiant struggle. I tried to hit him in the head, but he grabbed my hands.

"You want to play rough?" He grinned down at me, his teeth white in his dark face, and his eyes glowed a dangerous dark green.

A frisson of fear coursed down my spine. What did he have in mind? I kicked frantically and tried to free my hands.

"Enough!" He threw me onto the mossy ground in a small clearing.

Before I could struggle to my feet, he'd come down on top of me, straddling my waist, my wrists still imprisoned in one of his hands. He thrust them high above my head, arching my body upwards into his.

"What are you going to do?" I couldn't keep the fear from my voice.

There was something intense and wicked in his expression. I bucked under him, trying to throw him off me, but he was much too big, too heavy. I looked down and saw the bulge protruding from his slacks where he sat on my belly. My eyes flew back to his.

"You know what I want." His voice was a deep rasp and his free hand came up to rub over my breasts.

He swiftly untied the ribbon that held the bodice of my day dress closed. With a flick of his hand, my breasts were bared once more to his gaze. His eyes blazed brighter and he licked his hard sensual lips with the tip of his tongue.

"I have to taste you again," he said.

My good intentions flew out the window as he shoved one hard thigh between my legs and thrust them wide apart, spreading the full folds of the day dress aside. He lowered his erect groin onto mine and bent to seize one nipple in his mouth. One hand kept a firm grasp on my wrists, the other began squeezing and pulling on my other breast.

There was nothing I could do but lie beneath him as his mouth and hand moved relentlessly over my bare breasts. His penis was a hot and dangerous presence jammed against the side of my inner thigh. My breasts burned under his ceaseless attention, the pleasure almost pain as he squeezed and bit and rubbed them.

"Thomas!" I gasped, unable to keep from squirming against him.

The moisture flowed like a river between the crease of my ass and God forgive me but I wanted him buried inside me, like James, but so unlike him. I was desperate to feel him inside me.

He released my hands and knelt between my widespread legs. I fisted my hands in the soft mossy grass beneath me as I watched the slow smile kick up the corner of his sinfully wicked mouth. One of his hands continued to cup and squeeze my full breast. His other hand slowly pushed the skirt of my day dress up and I forgot to breathe as I felt the cool morning air waft over my exposed thighs.

"What are you going to do?" I whispered, feeling the heated blush fire my face as he pushed my underwear aside.

His eyes were on what he was doing and I watched as he brought that large hand to rest on the delicate hair between my thighs. Was he finally going to breach the walls of my filial commitment? I couldn't let him.

"Stop!" I cried out and placed my hand on his.

"Not yet," he said, his voice gone hoarse and husky.

"Oh heavens!" The exclamation came unbidden as I watched and felt him slide one long finger into me. I released my hold on him and fisted the folds of my skirt in my hands. The image was too intense, too erotic, and the sensations even more so.

"Do you like that?" He groaned and leaned over me once more.

He watched my eyes as his one hand squeezed my nipple hard, and he sunk another finger into my moist depths. Before I could object, he was sliding his fingers out, slick with moisture, but then he slid them back in.

I gasped and bit my lip, unable to tear my eyes from his intense green ones. They were dilated almost black and his face was dark with male need and desire.

"Let it happen," he said and his thumb came up to press on the extremely sensitive junction of my thighs.

The violation was too much, the relentless fondling of my breast and the magic of his fingers working inside me, on me. I tried one last time to think of James and object.

"No!" I cried, and twisted my head away so that I would no longer see those probing eyes staring so intently at me, but his hands didn't stop and the wild sensations were building so fast there was nothing I could do.

"Let me pleasure you," he said and lowered his mouth to my other breast.

Oh God forgive me, but it was all too much.

His teeth bit my breast, his hand squeezed my nipple hard, and his other hand rubbed mercilessly against me as he thrust his fingers rhythmically within me once more.

I screamed, helpless in the release that ripped through me.

When I opened my eyes again, I found Thomas leaning over me, watching me.

"Are you satisfied?" he smiled.

I nodded, flushed and ashamed that he had so pleasured me. I would never admit to him that James had not once succeeded in drawing such a response from me, though I intuitively grasped that this was what Thomas sought.

"I have pleasured you four times. Would it be too much if you were to grant me some release?" He looked down at me, his eyes still dark with desire.

I knew that what he was asking was sensually fair, but the whole situation was immoral. I could not in good faith consent to actions that violated my marital contract with his brother.

"No, I must not," I said and tried to sit up.

Thomas easily pushed me back down. He grabbed my hands again and thrust them over my head. I stared up at him in shock and surprise that he should deny my order.

"Sir, I said that I must not!" The fear was back. He was so big, so strong, he could do anything to me and I would be helpless to stop him.

"But I insist," he said and sat heavily once more on my belly.

I watched in terror as he unloosed the laces of his pants and gasped as he freed himself. I had not once seen my husband's penis when it was erect, though I had felt it against and inside me many a time. Still, that did not prepare me for the sight of Thomas's enormous cock rising from his open pants.

God, the thing looked as big as any stallions. I gulped. How would it ever fit within me?

"No, please!" I looked up at him, begging him to spare me.

Whatever pleasure I'd felt had winged away on the fear I felt at seeing such a monstrously large member. I watched paralyzed as he spit into his palm and then rubbed the moisture on the long broad length of him.

"What are you going to do?" I couldn't keep the quaver of fear from my voice.

"Don't worry, I won't compromise you." He released my hands and seized my breasts between both of his.

He pushed them together tightly and then thrust his penis into the crease they formed. The saliva worked to lubricate the passage of his penis. His fingers resumed their rubbing and squeezing of my nipples as he slid his penis rhythmically between the tight crease of my breasts.

"No, stop!" I had to prevent him from having his way with me. My hands were free and I reached up and tried to strike his shoulders.

"Get off me!" I cried.

"Not yet," he said.

He sat up and grabbed my hands.

"You need to behave." He pulled twine from his pocket and bound my hands. "You will behave. I told you, I will not compromise you." He forced my hands over my head once more.

"No, please," I moaned as he resumed thrusting his enormous turgid length between my breasts. The torment he inflicted on my nipples set them once more on fire and I watched in helpless fascination as he knelt over me. His eyes were dilated black and focused on seeing himself move between the large mounds of my breasts. The sensations began to build again and I squirmed, scissoring my legs as I felt the moisture seeping down my thighs again.

"Yes, oh yes," he groaned, his hips thrusting forward in a hard, fast rhythm as his fingers flicked and squeezed my nipples.

It was too much.

My body spasmed with pleasure and then I saw his climax rushing down upon him. His face was dark red, sweat beading his forehead and his upper lip, and I looked down just in time to see white liquid squirt free of the massive blunt head of his penis where it lay jammed between my breasts, anointing my neck and the mounding tops of my bosom.

"Thank you," he exhaled.

In moments, he had redone his pants and released my hands from their bonds.

I sat up quickly and shook out my skirts. With shaking hands I clumsily tried to lace up my bodice.

"Let me." He brushed my hands aside and laced me up, but not before cupping my full breasts once more in his large hands and squeezing my nipples.

Helplessly, I felt the fire burn though my veins.

"You are fantastic," he said and rubbed his thumbs across my erect nipples.

Heaven help me, but I stood powerless to move away from the magic of his hands. He watched my expression and grinned.

"You little liar. You want it as much as I do," he said and dropped his hands.

Before I could stop myself, I looked down and saw that once more his pants protruded. I shivered with fear and if I dared admit it desire when I remembered what lay hidden there.

"You and I are not finished. Not by a long shot," he said and turned away, disappearing into the woods.

I hung my head in shame as I returned to the formal gardens. So much for all my vows and promises to myself that I would respect my commitment to James. All I had to do was think of Thomas, and my body made a mockery of my marriage.

***

Chapter 4 - Marital Bliss

"You look radiant, my sweet." James kissed me lightly on the lips when he arrived the next day.

I embraced him with something close to desperation, knowing that Thomas stood nearby with my family watching our reunion.

"I'm so glad to see you again," I said and turned my face up to his once more for a kiss.

He obliged and I quickly opened my mouth, hoping he would take the hint. I felt him pause a moment, and then his tongue moved gently between my lips. His arms tightened against me and I felt his penis rising against my belly.

Thank heavens, I thought and returned his kiss fervently.

"Come now, you two, it's not as if you haven't been married for a while!" James's father, Charles, strode up laughing and James pulled away from me.

He smiled shyly and I saw the heat in his blue eyes. I vowed to myself that tonight, I would make sure that I received as much pleasure from him as possible.

It was a full house at Haven Home that week. All of my family was there as well as James's. In light of it being summer, dinner was a picnic affair out on the terrace above the gardens. A band played and after dinner there was dancing on the lawn.

"I've missed you so much," James said to me when he took me in his arms for the next dance.

"I have missed you, too," I sighed, happy to feel safe and secure once more in the arms of my husband.

We danced with each other, and then as tradition required, we danced with our other family members. As was expected, I had to dance with Thomas. He took the opportunity to pull me hard against him and gone was the feeling of safety and security as if it had never been. He eyed me hungrily, his green eyes dipping from my face to the deep cleavage of my gown.

"I love your breasts," he said softly.

And if on cue, I felt them erect against the soft fabric of his shirt. It was a warm evening and all of the men had discarded their coats for the more informal apparel of their shirtsleeves. A wicked grin curved his mouth, and I could tell he felt my response.

I breathed a sigh of relief when the dance was over and I returned to the safety of my husband. As the night drew on, I grew warm from dancing and went to the table set on one side of the lawn where the punchbowl was. The table was set back behind a low hedge and out of direct view of the garden. I held a cup and picked up the pitcher to pour a cup of punch when two big hands closed over my breasts. I almost spilled the punch as I shakily set the cup and pitcher back down.

"Thomas, let me go." I spoke quietly, aware that at any moment, one of our family members might appear on the scene.

His only response was to tighten his hold on my breasts, his large hands warm and firm, pulling me back against him at the same time that his palms rubbed over my distended nipples.

"You want this, you know you do," he whispered against my ear, his lips teasing the delicate lobe and he sensually bit down as his thumbs and forefingers grasped and then squeezed my nipples firmly.

Maybe it was the surprise of the assault, but for a moment, I forgot everything but the feel of him touching me, the wildfire of sensation he was pulling from my breasts, breathing into my ear. I could feel the hard stab of his massive shaft against the small of my back and my knees weakened in helpless response. And then I remembered.

"No, you mustn't!" I tried to twist away.

His fingers did not immediately release my nipples and the pleasure became almost pain as I tried to pull free. And then I was.

"Let me pour you some punch." Thomas was instantly at my side, pouring a glass of punch, and I found myself looking up into the loving eyes of my husband.

"There you are, my dear," James said and dropped a light kiss on my lips.

I had to get away! It was too much to be standing between the two brothers, knowing how much they each desired me.

"Thank-you," I said as blandly as I could to Thomas, not meeting his eyes, and taking James's hand in mind, I pulled him back to the gardens.

"Do you mind if we retire now?" I asked a few minutes later.

I couldn't stand another moment of Thomas watching us. I felt his intense green eyes on me wherever I went and I knew by the light in them that he was still deeply hungry and unsatisfied in his desire for me. The very thought weakened my knees.

"Have you missed me?" James said later as we undressed in the bedroom.

Unlike our mansion in the city, Haven Home did not have separate changing rooms, and tonight, James sent my maid Hetty and his manservant away.

I turned and smiled shyly at my husband. I had never seen him completely naked before, and his eyes were just as eager to study my naked form.

"Yes, my husband, my love. I have longed to be with you again," I said.

He was tall and beautiful. I admired how his sparse chest hair arrowed downwards to his manhood. It stood erect from the dark nest of hair at the juncture of his thighs, a dusky red. It did not fill me with fear or trepidation. It was nothing like Thomas's massive staff. I looked up and saw that James's blue eyes were on my breasts.

"I can't believe we have never been like this together," he said and came closer. "You are so beautiful."

He stood beside me, his eyes fixated on my breasts as his hands came up to touch them. I shivered in response. My nipples were still tender, almost sore from how Thomas had used them earlier, and my nipples instantly erected against his palms.

"Oh, Sarah, I want you so much." James pulled me close and I reveled in the feel of our naked bodies touching from thigh to chest. His penis pulsed swiftly against my belly.

"Kiss me," I said and James lowered his mouth over mine.

Gone were the tentative kisses of our first encounters. His tongue thrust eagerly into my mouth and I returned his kiss with ardor. We went to the bed and I lay back, looking up at him with all the love I felt for him in my eyes.

"I can't believe how lucky I am," he said and climbed between my willing thighs.

I took his hand and brought it to my breast. He needed no other urging but began to stroke it, cup it, measure its fullness in his hand. I positioned my hips under him and he thrust easily forward into my warm body.

"You are so wet," he gasped against my ear and stilled his movement inside me. He propped his elbows beside my head and looked down at me.

"I have missed you so much. My body needs you," I said and kissed him again.

He responded wildly, his hips thrusting his penis deeper into me and he lay heavily on top of me.

"Oh Sarah!" He cried out and his thrusting reached a rapid tempo.

The sensations began to build. My breasts jammed against his bare chest and rubbed against his chest hair, erecting to aching peaks. The sensation was exquisite and I gasped as I felt a rush of moisture coat his shaft as he slid in and out of me.

And then he shuddered massively. I felt his seed shooting deep inside of me and he collapsed against me, his breath hot and rapid against my forehead. His penis still rested deep within me. I rolled my hips, frustrated, knowing that I had come close to ecstasy but it had not worked, not like with Thomas.

"That was incredible," James said and kissed my cheek.

He withdrew himself and rolled to lie on his back, drawing the covers up to cover his naked body. His eyes fluttered closed. "I am tired," he sighed. "It has been so busy with Father."

I ignored the frustration tensing my body and perched myself on my elbow and looked down at my husband. He did look tired and I felt sympathy for him.

"My poor man," I said, and lightly stroked my hand over the light fur covering his chest.

"Mmmm, that feels good," he said and opened his eyes.

They glittered and I could see the desire lighting them once more. I stroked my hand lower down across the silky fur of his belly and it brushed the warm tip of his erection pressing upwards.

"Oh Sarah!" His hand clamped down on mine and I wrapped my fingers around his hard flesh, feeling its steely strength and the swift pulse of his heartbeat engorging it with blood.

The next thing I knew, he rolled me on top of him. My breasts hung down, two big globes teasing his lips, and he needed no further urging but began to suckle first one and then the other.

"James," I sighed and braced myself above him.

His hands closed over my hips and he slid me up slightly. I felt him probe once more at my opening, still wet from his seed.

"Yes!" He thrust upwards, his penis filling me, his mouth swallowing hugely around my breast and I felt his tongue whip across my distended nipple.

"Oh James!" I cried as I felt lightening flash through me and my moisture added to his own, his penis sliding rapidly up into me.

I used my knees and increased the tempo. My breasts swung back and forth and his hands forced my hips to hold still as he penetrated me more deeply. The sensations built, on and on, he lasted much longer than before. He arched upwards and kissed me, his tongue thrusting wildly into me as his hands held me steady while he penetrated me vigorously below. My breasts slid erotically over his chest, now wet with sweat, my nipples hard diamonds of sensation.

Sensation built on sensation and the tempo increased even more. I thought I would die from pleasure, when suddenly wild spasms shook me from my head to my feet and I convulsed, collapsing against James.

"My dear, are you OK?" he said moments later when our breaths began to slow.

I still lay against him, my breasts mounded against his chest and I felt his penis slowly sliding free of my body. He moved out from under me and looked with love and concern at me. He lightly stroked my breast and smiled a very male smile when the nipple erected once more.

"Yes, I am fine. Better than fine. Do you think we made a baby tonight?" I asked looking up at him with glazed, satisfied eyes.

"I sure hope so," he murmured and pulled me close.

I fell asleep in his arms, feeling happier than I ever had. My husband had made love to me, I had achieved ecstasy, and maybe we had finally managed to conceive.

I thought for sure that after the night James and I had shared that my lust for his brother was cured. In the morning, James smiled his sleepy, sexy smile and climbed over me. Gone was the hesitation or the reserve. He feasted on my breasts, his hands roved at will over me, and he thrust into my eager, ready body. I tasted ecstasy with him again that morning such that when I headed down to breakfast an hour later I was sure I was immune to Thomas.

The day was spent with our families. We played croquet on the lawn and ate cucumber sandwiches with iced tea for lunch. Throughout it all, I felt Thomas's scorching green glance, but I refused to acknowledge him and told myself he meant nothing to me.

That night, we all boarded an assortment of carriages and open-covered buggies and headed to a neighboring estate for a party. I knew that James and his father had business to transact with the host and I knew it was inevitable that Thomas would hunt me down.

I managed to avoid him for most of the evening, though I could feel his eyes following me. The night drew on and Mama, my sister and the other youngsters returned to Haven Home. James finally sought me out.

"I'm sorry, my sweet, for being so absent this evening." He pressed an intimate kiss on the side of my neck and I let out a sigh. "But the business is going well. It may take a few more hours. Thomas has offered to give you a ride back home, if you'd like."

Thomas? No!

"No, I'm fine. I would rather just wait for you." I snuggled against his chest and kissed his jaw.

"Ah, how I wish we could just go home now, to bed," he said and pulled me closer, his hands resting on my hips. He looked down, his blue eyes filled with love and caring and desire. "You look tired, especially after all of our 'activity.'" He smiled intimately. "I insist. Thomas," he called to his brother who just happened to be passing by. "Will you please take Sarah home? Father and I have more negotiations we need to finish with Townsend and I don't want her to wear herself out."

I couldn't look at Thomas. I kept my eye on his cravat rather than meet his eye as he replied. Of course he was more than happy to take me home. There was nothing I could say. If I objected any more strongly than I had, James might suspect something.

James gave me a quick kiss and was gone.

The next thing I knew, Thomas had clamped a steel arm around my waist and escorted me from the room.

"You have been avoiding me," he said as soon as we were ensconced in his closed carriage.

He pulled the curtains and turned to me. I moved as far away from him as I could on the velvet cushions.

"Cutter is my man. He minds his own business." Thomas slid onto my seat and crowded close to me.

He didn't have to clarify. I knew that I was completely at his mercy. Even if I screamed, Cutter would do nothing. Irrationally, I felt excitement pulse through my veins. My nipples erected almost immediately against the fine silk of my gown.

"Thomas, you must understand. I am happily married to your brother. I love him. I do not want to compromise my relationship with him or cause problems between the two of you."

"Tisk, tisk." Thomas hauled me onto his lap.

He turned me to face away from him and I gasped as he seized my breasts once more in his large hands. "You protest too much." His tongue traced the curve of my ear and his hands began their merciless torment once more on my breasts. "Relax." His voice was a hiss causing frissons of sensation to course down my spine. "Enjoy the ride." He cupped my breasts and began squeezing my nipples hard through the silk of my bodice.

"Thomas!" I gasped, and humiliation flooded through me as I felt my body heat to his caresses.

I squirmed on his lap and felt the enormous length of his erection pressing against my back.

"You want me, you cannot deny it." He lowered the bodice of my gown and suddenly his hands were on my naked breasts. "Let go and feel. Yes."

He noticed how I squirmed against him. One of his hands traveled down and began bunching the skirt of my gown upwards. He licked and bit the side of my neck, his other hand moved back and forth between my breasts, squeezing and tugging at my nipples. My breath hitched in my throat and I felt moisture flowing between my thighs.

"I can never get enough of your breasts. They set me on fire." He continued to touch and tease my breasts. My gown was up around my hips and his hand crept around and stroked me below.

"You must stop, Thomas. Please. What would your brother say?" I said the words almost desperately as I felt one long finger and then a second slide into my moist core.

I couldn't help the way my nipples instantly beaded to diamond points as his thumb rubbed the sensitive nub at the juncture of my thighs.

"James won't know, so he'll have nothing to say. I certainly won't tell him, and I'm sure you won't risk your marriage, either."

I gasped in helpless frustration and desire as his hands shifted to my hips for a moment. Suddenly my gown was bunched around my waist and my bottom was bare against his groin.

"What are you going to do?" I said, fearful once more as I realized how completely under his control I was.

"Don't worry, I won't risk impregnating you."

With one violent rip, Thomas tore my underwear from me. Fear took over and I struggled wildly to get off his lap.

"Let me go!" I cried out and struggled some more.

"No," he said implacably, his large hand grabbing my wrists and holding them captive against my belly.

I felt him fumble behind me and then I felt the hot massive heat of his shaft directly against the bare flesh of my ass.

"Please, don't do this," I said and tried to scoot away from his groin.

"You want it. I'll show you how much," he said against my ear, his voice a husky rasp.

The hand holding my wrists yanked me backwards and I felt his staff embed itself between the tight lobes of my ass.

"Now be a good girl and behave." His breath came rapidly against my neck.

One hand still held me captive, but the other came around and pulled my legs wide to straddle him. He released my hands, wrenched my legs even wider across his thighs, and he leaned over me slightly. It was everything I could do to stay upright. I braced my hands on his rock hard thighs as one of his hands began to stroke my breasts again. The other hand cupped me below and once again his fingers sank into me.

"There, isn't that better?" He bit my neck lightly and I writhed helpless to deny the sexual tension building in my body.

His hand on my breasts, the other teasing and tantalizing me below, the massive girth of his shaft sliding slowly between the lobes of my ass as the carriage swayed.

"Relax. Let yourself go."

He increased the tempo and I began to moan, helpless in my body's response. His thumb teased the sensitive nub and suddenly white lightening shot through me and I collapsed against him.

"Yes," he grunted and his hands closed over my hips.

He pulled me back against him even more firmly and then raised me up and down as I felt the long hard length of his shaft sliding rapidly between the lobes of my ass. His breath came in short spurts and then suddenly he let out a groan and I felt moisture coating the bare flesh of my ass. He had spilled his seed on me once more.

Reality returned and I struggled to right myself.

"Just a minute," he said, amusement lacing his voice. "Let me clean you up." He took a handkerchief from his pocket and wiped away the moisture.

As soon as I could, I clambered off his lap and pulled my gown back into place. He adjusted his pants and watched me, his green eyes glowing with wicked pleasure.

"You are such a delight, Sarah. When will you admit how much you enjoy our interludes?"

"Never!" I said and breathed a sigh of relief as the carriage pulled up to Haven Home.

Before I could leave the carriage, Thomas grabbed my chin hard and stared deep into my eyes.

"You can't refuse me, my dear. You see that if you do, I will have to tell your brother that you have been throwing yourself at me."

"But that's a lie!"

"Then how do you explain this?" His mouth swooped down over mine and his tongue instantly thrust against my closed lips.

I refused to open to him, but he pulled me across his lap and settled his hands on my breasts, his fingers working their will on me. I gasped and his tongue thrust deep inside. I shuddered, unable to stop the longing that coursed through my body. He set me aside with a smug look on his face.

"See? You cannot deny that."

I stumbled from the coach, unable to contradict him. The evidence was clear in my dilated eyes and the aching peaks of my breasts that longed once more for his exquisite torment.

The next day as I feared, James had to return to the City for business. I clung to him when we parted, but there was nothing I could do. Both our families were leaving, but Thomas still had ranch business to conduct at Haven Home.

"I will see you soon, my sweet," James said when he kissed me goodbye.

I watched his coach leave with shaking knees and a fearful and yet excited dread of what Thomas might try next. I knew that his advances were becoming bolder and I shuddered in trepidation. So far we had not committed adultery, not in the correct sense of the word, and I wondered how long he would restrain himself.

My God! The thought of his massive staff impaling me filled me with fear and a sense of desperation. He wouldn't do such a thing, would he? I couldn't allow myself to bear a bastard child.

I went about my business the next day and went down to the stables to visit Nick. I was surprised to find the stable hand nowhere around. I should have realized the warning sign, but stupidly, I did not. I was happily grooming Nick when I heard the straw rustle behind me. I spun around, startled, expecting to see Thomas again.

Instead, Cutter stood there, a malevolent grin on his face.

"What are you doing? Where is Thomas?" I instinctively backed away from him.

"He sent me to you ma'am," Cutter said. "I'm to bring you to him."

"No, that is impossible. Please leave me." I used my most imperious tone.

Cutter simply smiled his malevolent grin. "My master says you must come, so you must come."

Cutter was a massive man. As broad as he was tall. Perhaps not as tall as Thomas, but definitely as broad and brawny. I gulped and looked about desperately for an escape. No such luck. He lumbered inexorably closer. Nick sensed my unease and whickered.

Suddenly, without warning, Cutter grabbed my arm and hoisted me toward him.

"You can't do this!" I shrieked.

Cutter clamped a hand over my mouth. I struggled furiously, but he'd lifted me off the ground and my feet had no purchase. I tried to kick him, but his hands held me like a steel vise against his solid body.

"I won't hurt you, ma'am, if you won't hurt me," he said.

Moments later, he thrust me inside one of the stalls at the far end of the barn. I stumbled. When I regained my footing, I gasped in surprise and fear. Thomas stood at one side of the stall, a hungry, wicked look in his eyes.

"Close the door, Cutter," he said.

Ropes hung from the ceiling.

"Bind her."

"No!" I spun around and tried to reach the door.

Thomas was faster, grabbing me from behind and hoisting me off my feet.

"Easy there, Sarah. Don't worry. We will all have a good time."

I struggled even more frantically when I saw Cutter approach, but Thomas's hands were steel bands on my wrists. I was helpless to do anything as Cutter attached the straps to my wrists and then cinched my arms upwards overhead.

"Now, Cutter, you can watch and await my command."

Thomas released my hair from its braids and then set to work on my riding habit.

"I swear, Thomas, I will scream if you continue with this insanity," I pleaded as he began unlacing the ribbons of my corset. I saw Cutter touching himself through his breeches and I shuddered. The lust on his face was an open book.

"Go ahead and scream, if you want," Thomas said. "I gave the stable hand the day off. The barn is completely empty except for us and animals who cannot talk."

"Please, if you feel anything for me, Thomas." My voice quavered and I felt close to tears as my chemise dropped away.

Thomas stood in front of me and stared at my naked body, exposed completely to his eyes as well as Cutter's rapacious gaze. I blushed and blushed again to feel their eyes on me. The humiliation, the shame was extreme. How could he do this to me! And with the hired help?

"You are a work of art. My brother is a lucky man," Thomas said and came forward, his hands seizing my breasts and cupping them. Cutter snickered. "See how big she is, she overflows my hands." Thomas spoke to his man and I felt rage sweep through me even as my nipples beaded against his palms.

"She be a ripe plumb one, indeed," Cutter agreed and touched himself some more.

"How dare you treat me like some kind of common whore!" I tried to twist away from him but my arms were tied tight above my head.

"Never a common whore. Never." Thomas cupped and squeezed and rubbed my breasts.

I closed my eyes, embarrassed by my body's obvious reaction to his touch.

"Don't be embarrassed, Sarah. You are gorgeous, spectacular. I want to give you ultimate pleasure. That is why Cutter is here. He will help me pleasure you."

"No, please!" I'd vowed I wouldn't beg, but the idea of the other man touching me was revolting.

"I have an idea. This should help you relax and give you over to sensation."

My eyes flew open but too late when I realized he had tied a silken sash around my head. I could see nothing.

"Thomas, please, you can't do this!" I cried, struggling to free my arms from the bonds but to no avail.

Hands closed over my breasts. I had no idea if they were Thomas's or Cutter's. They were large and warm and began cupping and rubbing my nipples. I thought it might be Thomas because soon they were tugging and squeezing my nipples to almost painful awareness. I squirmed in spite of myself. Sensual heat flooded my body.

"Give yourself over to sensation, Sarah, let us show you how good it can be." Thomas's lips moved against my neck and another set of hands began stroking my hips, sliding down to cover the junction of my thighs, fingers sliding into me.

THE COMMANDMENT

A mouth closed over one of my nipples and a tongue lathed me. Another hand continued its torment of my other breast. Another hand sank itself deep into my moist depths.

"That's better," Thomas said from somewhere behind me as my head sagged, rolling loose on my neck.

My knees gave way as desire swept through me and I felt his mouth on my neck once more. The sensations began to build with frightening speed. I couldn't believe what was happening, what Thomas and Cutter were doing to me, but my mind began to shut down and my body took over as their hands kept up their relentless sensual assault.

Big warm hands began kneading the bare lobes of my ass and I stiffened in surprise when a finger began to push into the tight bud of my anus.

"What are you doing?" I cried in shame and disgust, frightened when I found my body violently responding to the finger that sank deeper into my nether core.

"She likes that me thinks," Cutter said in front of me.

I realized it must be him working on my breasts. The thought did little to relieve me. My nipples had gone diamond hard at Thomas's perverse intrusion.

"She'll like this even more." Thomas's voice was a raspy growl when I felt his finger slide free.

It was replaced by a massive blunt object that pushed against my anus. I felt its heat and rapid pulsing and I knew that Thomas was planning to put himself inside me.

"No, you won't fit!" I cried and tried to move free of him, but Cutter's hands on my breasts held me in front and one of Thomas's hands was clamped firmly over my crotch, two of his fingers still buried in my moist depths, his thumb rubbing mercilessly against my clitoris.

"Relax, you will be surprised what can happen." His voice was an uneven gush of air against the side of my neck as I felt hands close under my thighs and lift me off the ground.

"No!" I cried and tried once more to struggle free.

Teeth closed over one of my nipples and the other hand squeezed hard on the other nipple. I knew without words it was a warning. I froze.

"That's better," Thomas grunted and I felt the massive head of his shaft push into me as he lowered me slowly, inexorably down upon him.

For a moment, Cutter's hands disappeared from my body. I held my breath in fear bordering on pain as my body stretched to incredible lengths to accommodate his massive cock.

"Please," I whispered and licked dry lips.

My body felt like it was being split asunder by the enormous, hot throbbing shaft violating my backside.

"Relax, we're almost there." Thomas's voice was unsteady, barely recognizable. "Yes!" He grunted and I screamed, unable to stop myself, as he suddenly rammed himself fully within me.

"Pleasure her, Cutter," Thomas gasped and I found myself sensually assaulted from all sides.

Hands and a mouth closed over my breasts, rubbing, licking, suckling, squeezing, tugging, drawing frantic moans involuntarily from my throat as another hand sunk one finger, two, more, deep into my front, and Thomas's massive shaft slowly withdrew and then surged into me.

"I can't take it!" I screamed again.

THE COMMANDMENT

The sensations were overwhelming. I thought I might die from the plundering of my backside, but then all the other sensations overrode the pain and discomfort. Electric arcs of sensation burst through my body and I screamed again as my body collapsed in ecstasy, held up only by the binds that tied me and by Thomas's penis impaling me.

"Yes, feel it, feel me, yes," Thomas grunted and thrust his massive shaft so deep I felt his balls brush the lobes of my ass. "Yes!" Warm gushing liquid shot deep inside me and I felt the convulsions pulsing all along the length of his massive shaft.

Something warm and sticky spilled across my breasts and I recognized the musty smell. Cutter must have spilled his seed as well. My knees gave way as Thomas withdrew his still rigid flesh from my backside.

"Here, let me help you." Thomas's arms swept around me. "Release her and leave us," he said to Cutter.

Moments later, the blindfold was gone and I found myself lying across Thomas's lap. He was fully clothed but I was still completely naked and my body felt used, dirty and yet blissfully satisfied at the same time.

"You were wonderful, amazing. God, I want you all over again." Thomas looked down at me, his green eyes fierce and hungry once more.

"Please Thomas, I don't think I can take much more." Unexpected, tears trickled down my face.

"Trust me. It will be much easier this time," he said and his hands moved over my breasts once more. "Let me pleasure you, just the two of us. Please." He dropped his head and lathed one erect nipple with his tongue.

Heaven help me but my body seemed to have a life of its own. Even after the indignities he'd forced me to suffer, I couldn't stop my body from instantly responding to his touch.

"You can't get enough, either, can you." He picked me up in his arms. I was too tired, too overcome to fight. "You'll like this, I promise," he said, his voice thick once more with desire as he draped me over a saddle bench, leaving my ass high in the air and my breasts hanging free down the other side. "Relax." His voice was a sibilant hiss and his hands once more began to stroke and tease my ass.

Another hand came around to cup and touch my groin. My breasts ached for touch and before I knew what I was doing, I had both my breasts in my hands, teasing them as Thomas had done to me so many times before.

"There you go, yes." Thomas folded his body over mine and the big blunt head of his cock once more prodded at my anus.

His hands came up to hold my hips steady and then he thrust his massive shaft slowly, smoothly into me. "Yes, yes, yes."

The words became a guttural litany as he pistoned himself, pushing in and then slowly pulling out and then thrusting himself so deep I felt his balls squash up against the plump lobes of my ass. His seed had made the passage smoother, slick.

He upped the tempo. I was panting, sweat beading across my body from the intimate violation. My body was shoved forwards and back as he thrust into me, my breasts swinging wildly. It was too much. His mouth was on my neck, his teeth biting the sensitive flesh just below my ear.

I screamed again as the climax took me and I melted over the saddle bench. But he was relentless, pistoning into me with greater and greater force.

I climaxed again, and then again.

I swear to God I felt like I would die from how deeply he impaled me on his massive cock.

I must have lost consciousness, because the next thing I knew, I was lying once more across his lap and he was kissing me gently on my temple, brushing my long hair out of my face.

"So beautiful," he said softly.

The room smelled of sex and unmentionable acts. I had to get out of there and away from him, but I felt too weak, unable to do anything but lie there quiescent in his arms.

"Let me take you back and tend to you."

He helped me into my clothes and unresisting I let him lead me back up to the house. He told Hetty that I'd taken a spill off my horse and that I needed to rest. He dismissed her and I found myself unable to object when Thomas stripped me once more and washed my body. I blushed when he touched me intimately and avoided his eyes when my nipples instantly beaded at the touch of the cloth against my ass.

"It is nothing to be ashamed of, how your body responds to me," he said.

I glanced at him and saw the latent hunger lurking behind his green eyes.

"But you must know that I have not compromised you to James. You cannot get pregnant from what we have done."

As if that would make it all right!

"Get some rest. I will see you later."

I had to get away from Thomas and his manservant. There was no way I wanted a repeat performance of what happened in the stables, even if my body had performed like a puppet on a string. Before nightfall, I had packed and had loaded my trunks and Hetty into the coach. We set off at a rapid pace for New York.

I had two weeks of married bliss, once more in the safe security of my husband's arms, before my relief was once again destroyed. Thomas arrived to conduct business with James. I studiously avoided him, but one afternoon, as I left the kitchen in the servants' quarters, a hand pulled me into a service room.

"Don't make a sound," Thomas said against my ear as he locked the door and pulled me into his arms.

I knew I could say nothing. There was no way I could risk the servants finding me with him. I was at his mercy, and God help me, for all the effort I'd taken to avoid him, I felt my body pulse to life as he kissed me deeply, passionately. Before I knew what I was doing, my hands were buried in his thick hair and his hands had dropped my bodice. I trembled with delight as his hands began their familiar yet breathtaking assault on my breasts.

"Please," I whispered.

"Yes," he breathed against my lips. "I must have you Sarah, now. It's been too long." He turned me around and threw my skirts over my waist. "Bend over," he rasped against my ear and licked it as he pressed his body over me, pushing me down across a table.

My heart leapt in my throat as I felt him fumble with his pants.

"God, how I want to make love to you." He groaned and I felt the massive head of his penis brush the curls of my moist femininity.

"No!" I jerked, trying to pull away from him.

"Don't worry, I won't endanger you," he said bitterly and then I felt him jam the thick head of his penis into the tight bud of my anus. "Relax," he grunted, his hands moving, stroking, kneading the lobes of my ass as he pushed deeper into me.

My breasts rubbed across the rough surface of the wooden table and my nipples erected. I had to brace myself against the table as he pushed ever deeper into me.

"Oh Sarah," he groaned and rammed himself full inside me.

One big hand covered my mouth just in time to prevent the scream from escaping my lips. The violation was so intense, so deep. I wasn't sure where pleasure ended and pain began. He slowly withdrew and then thrust into me once more. His mouth closed over my ear, he chewed, his breath an unsteady hiss as he pushed himself deeply into me and then withdrew.

Try as I might, I couldn't contain the sensations that began to lick like fire through my body. I didn't want to give him the satisfaction of knowing he had pleasured me, but it seemed it would never end, the steady, rending piston of his massive staff, stretching my backside to unimaginable widths, my breasts dragging across the table with each thrust, his mouth biting, licking, tonguing the sensitive flesh of my neck.

God forgive me, but I couldn't help it.

He thrust once more with mighty force and his hand crept up to tease and slide eager fingers into my front side. He felt the rich moisture soaking my thighs.

"Let it happen, Sarah," he grunted and began ramming into me, steadily, unceasingly, pushing himself deep and then deeper still, his fingers working their magic on the sensitive nub at the junction of my thighs, one long finger sliding into my moist depths

It was too much, my nipples scraping on the rough wood, his fingers buried in my moist depths, his massive shaft impaling me upon its enormous girth. I climaxed in mindless waves as I felt him simultaneously convulsing deep within me, shooting me full of his seed.

He withdrew and I collapsed against the table, uncaring that my skirt was still rucked up over my waist.

"Come, we must make haste." He pulled my dress down and took my hands, urging me to stand.

I looked up at him, disgust and shame and desire all racing through me.

"I didn't compromise you, Sarah, I honored our agreement." He pulled my gown up over my breasts, his eyes regretful as they disappeared from view.

"Our agreement?" I hissed at him. "I don't recall agreeing to any of this."

He nodded but I could see he knew I was only saying what I wanted to believe.

"I will leave first," he said.

Seconds later, I was left alone in the service room, standing on unsteady legs as I felt his seed slip free of my sorely used backside.

***

Chapter 5 - My Punishment

Another month passed and Thomas was gone on business. My own husband was absent much of the time as well, but I had something to keep me company and make me happy. I was finally pregnant with our much desired child. We were ecstatic and spoke eagerly about the future when we would be a family. I was lucky not to have morning sickness, and except for fatigue and some dizziness, I felt fine.

Imagine my surprise when one morning as I slept late, the door to my bedroom opened and I felt familiar hungry green eyes on me again.

"You are pregnant," he said and stood looking down at me.

I pulled the blanket self-consciously up to my neck. My breasts had grown ever larger since the pregnancy had begun and I did not want him to see.

"What are you doing here?" I said looking toward the door. "Hetty could walk in at any second."

"I locked it," he said and approached the bed. "You are pregnant," he said, almost as if he were speaking to himself.

"Of course, did you think that James and I never made love?"

He moved closer and gripped the coverlet in his hand. He began to pull it off me.

"What do you think you are doing?" I tried to keep my hold on the blanket but he suddenly, violently swept it away.

I was wearing nothing but a silken night robe and his nostrils flared as he took in my jutting breasts, quite visible through the thin cloth, my nipples grown large as they prepared for the babe.

"If you are pregnant, then we do not risk my giving you my bastard," he growled.

He could not be serious! Before I could react, he'd pushed me down onto the bed. He shoved my legs wide and pushed his groin against mine.

"Sarah, I have longed for this since the moment I met you."

"Stop it, stop it right now." I tried to wriggle free from him, but he grasped my hands in one of his big ones, his other hand shoved the robe aside and fastened on my breast as he dipped his head to kiss me, deeply, with a controlled fire that sent me squirming and writhing in helpless pleasure as I felt the sensuous lash of his tongue across mine, his penis pushing through the material of his pants against my tender and naked femininity, spread wide and open to him.

"God, you've grown," he groaned against my neck as he cupped and measured the swollen mounds of my breasts.

When his thumbs and forefingers began squeezing and pulling, tugging and rubbing my overly sensitive nipples, his penis prodding the sensitive junction between my thighs, I couldn't restrain the instantaneous climax. My body bucked and heaved and I would have screamed if his mouth hadn't been covering mine.

"You are incredible!" he whispered, his voice a deep rumble in his chest.

As I lay passive in the aftermath of my passion, I realized his hand had strayed to his pants and had released the long thick shaft of his manhood. My eyes flew to his as he climbed over me and teased the enormous blunt head of his cock against my moist passage.

"No," I whispered, but I couldn't tear my eyes from his.

I saw how they had dilated from green to almost pure black as he slowly squeezed the hot head of his cock into my tight sheath.

God, he was enormous. There was no comparison to James.

I bit my lip and held my breath as I felt my body stretch to accommodate his vast size, pain and pleasure mingling.

"You are too big," I shuddered with fear and then with longing, as I felt moisture lubricate his implacable penetration.

"For you, never." His voice was a throaty rasp as he jammed himself all the way to the hilt, his balls brushing against the lobes of my ass.

I gulped for air, feeling him fill me almost beyond capacity. His shaft pulsed swiftly, throbbing with a wild heat that stoked the fires within me. I felt moisture slide along his tremendous length.

"You like it, you know you do," he said, a hand coming up to tweak and torment my breast as he began to withdraw his turgid staff.

"Thomas," I moaned, unable to stop my body's response to his relentless sensual assault.

He closed his mouth over mine once more and I forgot everything as his tongue's rhythmic thrusting mimicked the steady surging of his massive cock into me. The pace continued and began to speed up. His stamina was incredible. I wasn't sure how much more I could take, my breasts rubbing relentlessly where they pressed into the smooth linen of his shirt. His hands fastened on my hips, holding me firmly as he rammed into me with violent force. I couldn't control the cascade of sensation that ripped through me. I screamed into his mouth once more and he let out a deep groan as I felt his cum shoot into me.

I collapsed back against the sheets, but minutes later, he turned me over.

"Kneel for me," he said against my ear.

I wasn't sure why I obeyed, except perhaps that my body still felt so languid from my release. The next thing I knew, he folded his body over me, his hands on my breasts, rubbing and squeezing, his penis pushing deep into me once more.

For an instant I remembered the other times he'd come in from behind, when he'd plundered the tight depths of my backside, but then there was no comparison.

My body was wet and willing and his giant shaft crammed into me with only a silken, sensual resistance.

"Oh Sarah," he grunted as he thrust into me, his hands working their sensual torture on my breasts.

Instantly, I came, unable to stop my body's wild response.

He thrust on, pistoning into me, the force of his thrusts pushing my face into the pillows, which was a good thing, because I came again, screaming. His hands left my breasts and fastened on my hips as he drove himself furiously into me, impaling me swiftly, relentlessly on his massive cock. My breasts swung wildly, my body jammed forward and back as he shoved himself into me and then withdrew, all the way to the blunt head of his enormous staff before surging into me once more.

God, would it ever end?

I thought I might explode, and I came again with such violent force that the world went black.

When I opened my eyes again, Thomas lay beside me, fully clothed, an arm across his eyes. I looked down and realized I was still uncovered, my body lying wantonly naked on the sheets. I started to pull my night robe over me.

"Don't," he said.

His green eyes met mine and they swept over my body, my breasts rosy and flushed from his attentions.

"You are so damned beautiful."

"Thomas, you have to get out of here." I looked fearfully at the door and sat up.

"You're right." He let out a sigh and ran a hand through his hair.

He looked at me with an expression I'd never seen coloring his face. He looked rueful. "Well, I guess it's official. We've now committed adultery."

Oh God, I'd completely forgotten!

I jumped out of bed and pulled the robe around me, tying it securely.

"Get out, get out!" My voice rose, almost hysterical.

"Don't worry, I'm leaving." Thomas slipped from the room.

When James and I next made love, I couldn't help comparing him to Thomas. Oh how the shame and guilt swept over me! There was no comparison.

And yet, as James brought me to a gentle climax with his mouth, I realized that this passion was something I could work with, something that didn't feel like it would rip me apart at any moment. I loved James, with all my heart, and our mating had made a baby inside me. That should be enough.

But the next time Thomas was in town, I couldn't stop myself from watchin99g him. I told myself it was because I was curious about the woman he had brought to visit. She was gorgeous, a spectacular redhead, and like me, she had big breasts. I could only imagine how Thomas sought his pleasure with her. That thought haunted me more than once as I saw them embrace and dance together at the various functions.

I told myself it was for the better that he had found someone else to focus his voracious appetite upon, but still, I couldn't stop watching him, remembering the feel of his hands on me, the intensity of him filling me, the wild and insatiable ecstasy I had found with him.

Just when I thought I'd made peace with the situation, I found myself alone with Thomas in the study. I had come looking for James.

"He has gone out on an errand." Thomas watched me, his green eyes predatory, and all the old feelings came rushing back.

"Where is Miss Townsend?" I said, looking about desperately for his fiancée.

"She is making a call to some friends." Thomas moved around me and locked the door.

"What are you doing?" I backed away from him, and yet I couldn't stop the wild surge of desire that made my knees weak and unleashed floods of moisture between my thighs.

"Pregnancy agrees with you." His green eyes dropped to the enormous mounds of my breasts.

They had grown to astounding proportions and they were so sensitive I had taken to wearing a full corset to keep my nipples from the endless sensual torment of rubbing against my gowns. I backed away from Thomas until the desk pressed against me.

"While the cat's away, the mice will play." He advanced suddenly and clasped me in his arms. "God, I've missed this," he sighed and buried his face in the curve of my neck.

His hands quickly undid the buttons of my dress and before I knew it, he'd pulled the strings of my corset loose. My breasts tumbled free.

"My God!" he gasped, his hands coming up to cup and shape my breasts, tracing the white mounds of my cleavage as he pressed them. His fingers rubbed and teased my nipples that were already distended and peaked with aching need.

"Oh, Thomas, you have no idea." I was instantly ready for him. I craved him, deep inside me, filling me once more with his giant staff.

He saw the desire sweep like lightening through me. He wasted no time but pushed me backwards across James's desk, impatiently sweeping the papers aside, and then he shoved my skirts up over my thighs. I was panting with need as he quickly freed himself from his pants and probed my cleft with the hot blunt head of his cock.

"Yes!" I gasped, swallowing convulsively, as he forced himself into me.

He was relentless, ramming his massive, throbbing penis into my moist tight core, splitting me wide as he squeezed himself inside, all the way to the hilt until his belly pressed against mine.

"Please!" I gasped again as he just as steadily began to withdraw, my body feeling emptied, a void, clinging desperately to his silken flesh as he pulled out.

I lay back on the desk and looked up at him, unable to tear my eyes from the intent hunger burning in his forest green eyes. I looked down and saw the vast thick girth of his turgid shaft where he shoved into me again, penetrated me, pinioned me, held me captive with his massive flesh. The sight was incredibly erotic and I moved my hips involuntarily.

He needed no encouragement. He surged into me, his hands on my thighs, spreading my legs even wider to accept his powerful thrusts. My breasts jerked back and forth, my nipples diamond hard points. Helpless in my desire, I reached up and pulled, rubbed, squeezed my nipples as he grunted and pistoned into me. The sensation was incredible, I wished he would never stop, but the tension built quickly, spiraling upwards and out of control as he rammed into me at a merciless rate, his hands like vises on my hips holding me steady as he thrust into me with mighty force.

"You want me, you want me, you want me," he chanted with each goring thrust.

I could not deny him. With each withdrawal, I panted, "Yes, yes, yes," and then it was too much, a thousand pulsations shattered me.

But he kept thrusting and I climaxed again, and then once more, biting my lip to keep the scream from alarming the servants, and then I felt him thrust once more, so deeply I felt as if he had reached my very soul.

Gushing jets of liquid shot into me and I felt the convulsions take him. He leaned heavily against me for a moment. I felt his heartbeat, rapid and swift against mine and down below where he still lay deeply penetrating me.

"Tell me to get off you," he said finally. "Tell me to stop."

"Get off me. Stop," I said, but without inflection.

I was too tired, too sated to do anything but lie there with him on me, in me. I felt his shaft begin to beat more heavily and his breath hitched in his throat.

"God, can you take more?" he rose up and looked down at me.

I met his gaze and then looked down to see his penis once more swelling, filling me with its promise of aching ecstasy.

"Once more, just once more," he groaned and began to withdraw and then thrust his engorged flesh into me.

This time seemed even more endless than the last. We were like animals locked in some kind of wild mating rite. He was dripping with sweat and lust. He did not slow the tempo as he unbuttoned and shed his shirt. I had never seen him unclothed before and the sight was breathtaking.

Just as he had tormented my nipples, I reached up and treated his to a similar attention. The action drove him wild. He surged into me, grunting, nothing more than his cock, and I whimpered, panting, urging him on, reduced to nothing more than sensation as my breasts peaked and I climaxed again and again, in pulsating waves.

In a final violent thrust, he collapsed against me, his mouth descending for a deep penetrating kiss as the orgasm ripped through his body.

He pushed himself off me and collapsed into the chair beside the desk. I got up and shakily sank into the chair on the other side. We were silent for some time as our bodies returned to earth. Finally, he spoke.

"I am to marry Miss Townsend next week. We have to stop this."

I pushed myself unsteadily to my feet, feeling my breasts hopelessly distend and erect without the support of my corset.

"Of course. It never should have been, Thomas. And soon I will be so great with child that I cannot risk such things. Can you help me?" I turned my back to him so that he could lace up my corset.

"I will miss you," he said, kissing my neck and running his hands one last time across the large mounds of my breasts. "I will miss these." He squeezed and rolled my nipples between his fingers.

"Oh Thomas," I let out a sigh.

We were back to square one and I was ready for him. He drew a deep breath and then his hands left me. The corset strings tightened and my breasts were once more restrained and safe from his dangerous attentions. I tidied my hair and minutes later, I was on my way back to my bedroom to cleanse myself before James returned.

I knew now that no matter how much we lusted for each other, Thomas and I could no longer continue our dalliance. I was to bear James's child and soon Thomas would have children of his own.

As I changed into fresh clothes and undergarments, I knew that the rest of my life I would suffer the punishment of remembering absolute ecstasy without the means to fulfill it.

But it was only fitting that I receive some punishment for having violated one of the Ten Commandments.

THE END

###

Did you love *The Commandment*? Then you should read *The Governess: An Erotic Regency Romance Novel*[1] by Loreli Love!

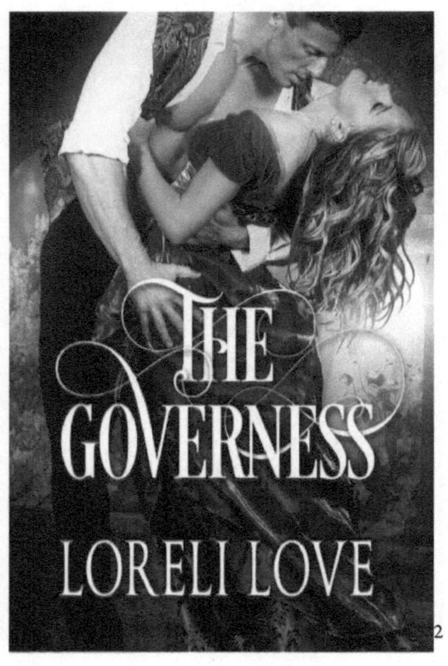

This fully developed 53,000 word novel is an erotic twist on *Jane Eyre*.

Young Clara Marsden leaves the orphanage to take a position as governess at a lonely English manor house on the moors, where highwaymen, mysterious standing stones, screams in the night, and handsome Mr. Robertson challenge her beliefs. Upon the destruction of Wereford Hall, her position as governess takes her to the verdant South of England where she encounters a

---

1. https://books2read.com/u/bWK8kG

2. https://books2read.com/u/bWK8kG

randy Earl and his lusty maids, and finally, she meets the man of her dreams who uncovers her destiny and birthright.

Read more at https://books2read.com/ap/8pL318/Loreli-Love.

About the Author

Loreli Love writes well-written erotic romance novels and stories that steer clear of the darker aspects of the human psyche. Her preference is for titillating delights, love, and happy endings that will bring sensual pleasure to her readers. She is the author of many erotic regency romance novels and other works, including The Earl's Lady, *The Education of Charlotte Royce*, *The Governess*, and *The Quartet's Quandary*, among others. All books are available in digital or print through a wide variety of vendors.

Read more at https://books2read.com/ap/8pL318/Loreli-Love.